CELLPHONICA

Chinese Tool helps gain World Domination

JASON O'NEIL

ISBN 978-1-957582-16-0 (paperback)
ISBN 978-1-957582-17-7 (eBook)

Printed in the United States of America

Books by the Author

Bald Eagle Vision

The Red Box

Turbopod

Turbospace

Sinecure

Cyberclipper

When Baldie Cries

New Age Ark

A Necessary Coup

Micronations

Hypersonica

Mission Embryo

DroneViper

Bald Eagle Vision 2

DragonChip

Cast of Characters

Dr. Mi Yan Cho
Chinese Virologist, Lab Director
Age 55
Intern at Mayo Clinic
Similar to: Ziyi Zhang, Chinese Actress

Dr. Wo Pon Tang
Virologist, Asst. Laboratory Director
Age 60
Graduate, Cambridge University, UK
Similar to: Man-Tat Ng, Chinese Actor

Mr. Wan Li-Kong
Test & Safety Director
Age 52
Graduate of UCLA, Los Angeles
Similar to: Chow, Yun-Fat, Chinese Actor

Mr. Kong, Mi Lei
Specimen Vault Manager
Age 48
Similar to: Jet Li, Chinese Actor

Mr. Lun, Kai-shek
President Ling's Chief of Staff
Age: 58
Similar to: Jackie Chan, Chinese Actor

Colonel Wan, Mo-Bei
Chemical Weapons Officer
Age 46
Similar to: Bruce Lee, Chinese Actor

Chow, Shendu
Medical Capsule Manufacturer
Age: 48
Chemical engineer, Penn State U.
Similar to: Stephen Chow, Chinese Actor

Feng, Woo Han
Cellphone Printed Circuit Board Designer
Age 51
Graduate, MIT, Boston, MA
Similar to: Fengyi Zhang, Chinese Actor

Mao Ling
President of China
Age 70
Former General in People's Army
Similar to: Zhou En-Lai, Premier of China

Hong, Tai-Tak
Supreme Commander, People's Army
Age 65
Similar to: Andy Lau, Chinese Actor

Ms. Mi Lan Po
US Intelligence Agent in Hong Kong
Age 42
Leads Underground network in China
Similar to: Kathy Park, TV Journalist

Andrew Ho
Mi Lan Po's Life Partner
Age 44
Internationally-acclaimed Architect
Similar to: Baotian Li, Chinese Actor

Vladimir Kolzou
President of Russia
Age 62
Studied in Heidelberg, Germany
Similar to: Vladimir Putin, Russian President

Greta Shiller
Secretary General, UN in Geneva
Age 60
Former German Chancellor
Similar to: Angela Merkle

Contents

Chapter 1: Ordos...1

Chapter 2: Dongguan 7

Chapter 3: Shenzhen...12

Chapter 4: Beijing...15

Chapter 5: Lot One 20

Chapter 6: Choibalsan 24

Chapter 7: Beijing II 30

Chapter 8: Hong Kong 35

Chapter 9: Tehran...38

Chapter 10: Hong Kong II 43

Chapter 11: Moscow...47

Chapter 12: New York City 54

Chapter 13: Beijing III...58

Chapter 14: Tamir Gol 62

Chapter 15: Geneva...66

Chapter 16: Hong Kong III 69

Chapter 17: Bermuda 72

Chapter 18: Cellphonica...75

1

Ordos

Three hundred and fifty miles west of Beijing is the largest ghost town in the world called Ordos. This ultramodern metropolis was built to attract 8-million people to a new work center in Inner Mongolia. In 2021 the city with its broad 12-lane boulevards, modern civil buildings and high-rise apartment buildings as far as the eye could see, stands deserted with only about 100,000 inhabitants. High rent, taxes and shoddy construction deterred millions of Chinese from moving there. The city is near some of the largest open pit coal mines in the world. But the miners are not urban dwellers. Thus, the eerie emptiness of the sea of concrete is home to only a handful of bribed citizens. Indeed, the city is so empty that the American, Matt Flynn, used it to develop his famous Turbopod vehicle which combined the car, airplane, helicopter and boat and required urban use regulations be developed for certification in the United States.

Twenty-six miles south of Ordos at the end of a deserted highway is the monument to the most famous Mongolian in history, Genghis Khan. This white marble, 2-story building is the leader's mausoleum. In truth, however, the stone casket is empty. The Khan, who ruled the world from the Pacific Ocean to the Caspian Sea between 1188 and 1226, is buried in the mountains west of the city, and historians believe that he ordered 1,000 horses to remove any trace of the long, dusty funeral procession. The monument, however, has a very sinister use as a hidden virology laboratory. Established and run by the Chinese military, this Top Secret facility develops and productizes lethal viruses used by the Chinese Communist Party (CCP) in its campaign to dominate the world.

Dr. Cho, Mi Yan directs a world-class virology laboratory containing state-of-the-art equipment reverse-engineered from vendors around the world. It contains 26 rooms under the parking garage. The 40-person staff is complete with two military liaisons. Above, guided tour groups act as cover for the laboratory which includes:

- Six development labs with vent pipes disguised at tree trunks
- Airtight containment areas including loading docks and specimen storage vaults
- Sterile test chambers
- Autoclave incineration facility

- Viral antigen and antibody detection sensors
- Sanitized, unisex air wash shower rooms
- Armed guards at the entry/exit points

The all-volunteer staff executes swear-to-secrecy documents. Violation results in physical harm to family members

-//-

This morning Dr. Cho has convened a meeting of her key staff members in a conference room. Participants include:

- Dr. Tang, Wo-Pon, Assistant Director
- Mr. Wan, Li-Kong, Test and Safety Director
- Mr. Kong, Mi Lei, Field Team and Specimen Leader
- Mr. Fu, Shen Wan, Industrial Liaison
- Colonel Wan, Mo-Bei, Assistant Director and Facility Manager

Sipping tea from sterile, capped porcelain cups, the team members were greeted by Dr. Cho:

"Good morning, Comrades, today I have a very exciting announcement and new assignment for our laboratory." She clicked a remote and activated a projector at the end of a long stainless steel table. A slide showed the summary of a Top Secret message from Beijing.

"Unit VL2626 is to leverage its current inventory of pathogenic viruses to develop a new strain which is 50-times more lethal than the Wuhan strain developed a couple of years ago. The lethality will be measured in vapor puffs per square foot. Conclusive, repeatable tests with video evidence will be provided within 6-months from today. Requests for resources of any kind will be honored for this National Priority Program."

This is directed by the Supreme Commander, General Hong.

Dr. Cho clicked off the projector and asked for questions. There were none. In silence, the team went to the specimen vault. Nobody said a word, but several reflected upon the incident in the city of Wuhan.

-//-

In the vault she asked her team to use the following specimens to develop the most lethal pathogens:

- Horseshoe Bats
- Pangolins
- Indonesian Monkeys
- Costa Rican Green and Black Frogs
- Vietnam's Bamboo Viper
- Wide Variety of Rats

She told the team: "Decide on the right 6 candidates, perform gain-of-function processes and down-select to 3 for particle atomization. Tests will be held with state prisoners."

They all nodded their consent.

-//-

Over the next four months, the team worked twelve or more hours per day. Some slept in a sanitized chamber. There were constantly monitored by Dr. Cho who would accept no failure. Outside the laboratory, in a sanitized lunchroom, she informed Colonel Wan of the progress on a weekly basis. Both the Doctor's and the Colonel's promotions depended upon this mission. During one of the meals, she described the development process:

- Inject a virus from a specimen into a host's cell cytoplasm
- The endosome membrane is fused by related RNA acid transferred from the cell's nucleus
- The modified RNA undergoes a protein synthesis creating a viral mass
- The mass grows on the cell where during incubation a proteolytic cleavage breaks the cell wall creating a new mutated virus
- The new virus reproduces in the infected cell

- Special agents accelerate the grow of the infected cells into a mass suitable for particle atomization

"Yes, Doctor, that is my understanding of the process," replied Colonel Wan. "So now what happens to these cells which have gained a more lethal condition?"

Dr. Cho reminded the Colonel of the Top Secret nature of the conversation and said: "Sir, here's where it gets very interesting. Our national leaders have devised a novel delivery scheme."

"Oh, and what is it?" asked the Colonel with a sense of urgency in his voice.

"Well, Sir, our mission to develop a virus so lethal that only a few whiffs of the gas form ingested through the nostril and/or mouth paralyzes major organs including the heart. Death of a person is measured in seconds, not minutes."

"Doctor Cho, why would anybody, and I mean ANYBODY, want such a thing to exist?" asked the Colonel.

"Sir, I can't answer that. I can only hope that somewhere, somebody develops a new antibody. The problem is that it would have to be administered immediately to be effective."

The Colonel nodded his understanding of the requirement and the impossibility of successfully treating somebody.

2

Dongguan

After a bullet-train trip from Ordos, Dr. Cho arrived in the ultra-modern metropolis of Dongguan in Guangdong Province north of Hong Kong. As she arrived at Shimbao, China's largest medical pill manufacturing company on the outskirts of the city, she was met by Mr. Shendu Chow, the company's President in the company's modern glass and marble lobby. Mr. Chow had applied his chemical engineering degree from Penn State University via the Safety Engineering career path. He has authored several books on assembly line sanitation during high volume runs of both hard and soft gel pill manufacturing.

"Dr. Cho, your reputation precedes you, and I'm so glad to finally meet and welcome you to our world!" said Mr. Chow as he vigorously shook the virologist's hand.

"You're most kind, sir," replied the intensely focused woman from Ordos. The couple then met several key members of the production staff in a large conference room just off the lobby. After the pleasant introductions and a sip of green tea, Dr. Cho opened the meeting.

"Gentlemen, my mission today is to review your manufacturing processes to ensure they are safe, and I mean VERY safe, to handle what we will ship here. I have the whole day and will report my findings this evening. This is a national program of supreme importance where schedules must be met. Failure is not an option. (Shibai bushi yi Zhong xuanze.)

"Dr. Cho," began the president, "we have been alerted to the importance of your project by Beijing. We understand and will fully comply with the strictest safety guidelines."

Dr. Cho quickly answered, "Sir, you are absolutely right. No employee here or elsewhere in our great People's Republic must be exposed to the contents of our shipments."

"I think you'll be pleased with our preparations through out your tour today." With that comment, the president nodded to begin the half-hour presentation detailing the production of hard and soft capsules with dangerous contents. Dr. Cho asked many questions and seemed satisfied with the answers.

-//-

For almost two hours the president served as the tour leader as the team walked the virologist through the hard gelatin capsule manufacturing process. Steps he highlighted included:

- Close acceptance inspection of the gelatin sheets
- Feeding of the sheets into the formation press where the sheets are melted into the capsule form.
- The movement of an encapsulated sheet through the filling and precise cutting press
- Joining of the two sides of the capsule via precise raised rings inside each half
- Leak detection
- Printing of the label on the capsule without disturbing the contents: liquid, gel or particle.
- Inspection with microscopes with lots sent to each in-house laboratory for testing
- Packaging of the capsules into blister packs or other retail transport vessel required by the customer.

Dr. Cho was quick to point out that the tiny capsules would be placed as input filters for the microphone on a printed circuit board in the end product.

Lunch was provided in the Executive Dining Room where several other key employees were introduced. The president took the time to praise the accolades of each person. Much of the discussion at the head table focused on the ability to maintain the 188F degrees of the sheets to form capsules. At the same time, the virologist alerted the team that the capsule had to be vaporized in 2-3 seconds.

As dessert and tea were served, President Chow announced: "My good Doctor, I have a real surprise for you which will be the first stop on our tour this afternoon."

The seasoned virologist chuckled and said, "You know, Sir, surprises in my business usually don't turn out well!"

Everyone at the table laughed while nodding their understanding of what was meant by her remark.

-//-

At 2:00 PM, the president led the doctor and several others down a long hallway and out the back door of the headquarters building. In the distance, about 200-feet away, was a pure white two-story building. The group walked under a covered walkway to the structure that looked quite sterile in the bright afternoon sunshine. The group entered the building and were escorted into a clean room for donning sterile suits, booties and clear visor headgear with small, lightweight, red oxygen pellet tanks on both sides. It was like visiting a spacecraft cleanroom but even more sanitary.

"This is quite a surprise, President Chow," said the virologist in a quite pleased tone of voice.

"This is gift from the People for your project," replied the president.

The group then met a young man who was introduced as the facility manager. He then proceeded to give a 40-minute tour beginning at the sterile loading dock with an air curtain to the warehouse to the redundant non-stop processing lines to the final inspection posts and laboratories. As the tour ended, the manager made several key points:

- This is a Top Secret facility with only cleared employees and a security control room to monitor the cameras, sensors and lockdown systems
- This small office is for the liaison personnel from Beijing
- This equipment senses any vapor release from the production lines. Should a release be detected, the headgear's oxygen supply is automatically activated as the employees calmly walk to a secondary cleanroom with detoxification stations.

At 4:00 PM, Dr. Cho shook hands with President Chow in the lobby. She ended her departure by saying: "Mr. Chow, I'm truly impressed. My report to the authorities will be positive. And we'll plan some trial runs in about 60-days."

As they walked outside, the president asked, "Can you tell me the final application or purpose of these capsules?"

As the virologist shook his hand, she said: "Sir, you'll know in due time. My lips are sealed." (Wo de zuichun bei feng zhule.)

3

Shenzhen

Colonel Wan landed at the ultramodern airport serving the city of Shenzhen located 50-miles south of Guandong and 12-miles north of Hong Kong on China's south coast. In the airport the colonel was met by an intelligence officer from Beijing. They shared a taxicab ride to the northern part of the city to an industrial park with dozens of factories which manufacture medicines and printed circuit boards (PCB's), typically used in cellphones.

The two officers entered the headquarters of Imagineering Inc, one of the largest PCB manufacturing companies in the world. In the lobby they were greeted by a Production Manager who introduced a senior PCB designer and the plant's security officer. The group then walked to a classified conference room where the obligatory hot teas were offered.

Armed with Dr. Cho's Trip Report from Dongguan and a stack of Orders from his commander, the colonel was very careful to discuss his requirements but not divulge the ultimate application for the PCB's under discussion. The intelligence officer nodded his permission to pass copies of the specification package across the table to their hosts. Over the next hour, the Imagineering team asked many questions, all of which were adroitly answered by the colonel. In summary, the company was to manufacture small quantities of PCB's which contained a proprietary, Top Secret, capsule designed to look like a power amplifier for a pinpoint microphone. An external signal would then cause the mounting plate to heat which would in turn immediately melt the capsule to release its contents as a vapor. This very novel requirement raised many questions for the engineers about the ultimate application, but no questions were asked. At lunch, the questions focused on the test requirements and the delivery schedule.

-//-

Promptly at 1:00 PM, the Production Manager led his guests to the end of the complex where, like Dongguan, a gleaming white building could be seen in the bright sunshine. Colonel Wan looked at the man from Beijing and just smiled. Only a few minutes later, the team was donning sanitation suits, being inspected and ushered through an airstream to a huge, pure white assembly area. As the team approached one of the glass windows of a cleanroom, the safety engineer proudly explained many of the features which eliminated contaminants.

He explained the complex series of vapor sniffers and sensors which would automatically halt production and alert the staff. The more the group moved from station to station, the more the colonel realized that his new friend from Beijing was instrumental in the design, build and operation of this facility.

Colonel Wan was clearly impressed by the numerous safeguards at the shipping and receiving dock to handle "sensitive" packages. And the personnel were trained to handle special containers with hazardous materials. It was also very clear that the dock personnel had no idea how special the new containers would be and the precise measures necessary to assure total integrity of the containers during the loading and unloading processes.

At the end of the day, the two visitors were escorted to the lobby and assured just how responsive Imagineering would be to the special project. Outside the building the two officers shook hands and took separate taxicabs.

On the plane trip back to Ordos, Colonel Wan wrote part of his trip report. He asserted that the delivery of the initial lot of the completed and tested cellphones would arrive at the mausoleum on schedule in sixty-six days. He noted that Beijing would have visibility of the entire process. The colonel smiled to himself at the prospect that somebody above him would be accountable for the success of the project, many aspects of which he did not have a Need-to-Know.

4

Beijing

On a cold, rainy morning in Beijing, a very important meeting took place with the President in the Forbidden City. The Chief of Staff. Lun, Kai-shek, welcomed his select, trusted leaders including:

- Chief of Staff of the Armed Forces
- Chief of Staff of Military Intelligence
- President, Shimbao
- General Manager, Imagineering Inc.
- Dr. Cho
- Colonel Wan
- Selected staff members with the highest security clearances

With President Ling seated at the head of a long, mahogany conference table and his trusted council members seated along one side of the table, Chief Lun led his visitors into the room to take their places at the other side of the table. After a couple sips of tea, the Chief warned the audience of the security classification of the discussion, and no cellphones would be allowed in the room

"Gentlemen and lady, this meeting is a very important milestone in our 5-year plan to control the Earth. With the astute guidance of President Ling, our nation has completed the first ten elements of project "Blue Planet." (Lanse Xingqiu)

A polite applause filled the room.

"On the slide projected on a screen at the end of the table, I have summarized the accomplishments in only four (4) short years." The Chief then briefly discussed each of the following:

- The installation of greedy and incompetent leaders in many countries who were required to ignore founding documents in order to create a Socialist State. (He chuckled at the ease of the transformation of the USA into the United Socialist Republic (USR).
- The creation of Welfare States around the world. National lockdowns were used to condition the masses to be subservient to the central government. People were paid not to work and thus be dependent upon the government for subsistence.
- The use of Debt Traps or loaned money in exchange for Chinese-controlled infrastructure projects such as highways, ports, petroleum refineries, harbors,

military bases and national communications systems. One project, the Silk Road Initiative (SRI) was billed as a route for commerce between Asia and Europe. The CCP viewed it as a superhighway for its invading military vehicles.

- The national wealth was driven out of a country by requiring state ownership of all property, confiscating profits, currency devaluation and rampant inflation to make the remaining money worthless.

- The outsourcing of manufacturing to China leaving low wage service jobs which accelerate personal and corporate bankruptcy.

- The use of Student Spies to steal critical technologies, particularly military, for these smart people to reverse engineer when the're forced to return to China. He remarked that there were 150,000 Chinese students in the USR alone.

- The Military Build-up. While major Western countries were required to reduce their military expenditures in order to fund the welfare programs, China vastly expanded its military on Earth, at sea and in space. The Chief took pride in China's ability to create an arsenal of nuclear-tipped, stealth hypersonic missiles safe in bunkers under the Great Wall. Fleets of modern submarines roamed the oceans at will.

- The control of the oceans including all canals and the new Polar Water Route in north Russia. This allows total control over the global supply routes.
- The control of Space with armed, stealth spacecraft positioned to knockout foreign communications satellite systems. An alternative to the GPS system was deployed as well as a military outpost on the Moon.
- The ability to defend against cyberwarfare. Many of the tools developed in the USR were stolen by the students and improved at home. The Chief was particularly proud that China had detected and neutralized the so-called "Dragonchips" developed in the old America to render Chinese in key positions "frozen-in-place" to prevent the launch of missiles. China developed an injectable metallic-ion fluid that masked the chips injected in the student's arms during the visa processing.

At this point, the Chief asked for questions and comments. There were none; only warm applause.

"Given the above, it is now time to fulfill China's destiny and execute project element number 11. Therefore, I ask for your attention to and support of this initiative which we will present in the next half-hour."

All principals nodded their consent.

In sequence, Dr. Cho, Colonel Wan, the President of Shimbao and the General Manager of Imagineering summarized the requirements and status of the progress in each of their domains. It was clear that the participants felt that the success of Number 11 was possible.

President Ling asked: "What is your test plan, and how soon could you report the results?"

The Chief looked at his team, and seeing no objection, stated: "Sir, we plan to use prisoners in Choibalsan to answer cellphones to receive a congratulatory call from you. We will report back in 60-days or less and be prepared to implement the final element of Blue Planet in six months."

The President looked at his advisors, found no objection and stood up and said: "Very well, proceed."

5

Lot One

"Dr. Cho, I think you'll be pleased with the results of the tests on Lot One," said a senior technician as the two people walked down the hall to the isolated testing chamber for new viruses. Colonel Wan joined the pair in front of a double-pane window at the end of a large chamber. A technician described the toxic vapor as a combination of a new virus with aggressive spike proteins for attachment to body cells combined with a mist of the most virulent poison extracted from a dreaded green frog from Costa Rica. The combination requires only a "short spritz" (like a common nasal spray) to immobilize the body's central nervous system.

As the trio peered through the window, a rat entered the chamber and immediately approached a smartphone with a piece of cheese on top. As the rat sniffed the cheese, a proximity sensor in the phone released two puffs of the new toxin. In about three seconds, the vermin was motionless on top of the cellphone. Colonel Wan looked at Dr. Cho and said, "Doctor

Cho you've done it! How soon do you think we'll be able to ship a lot to Dongguan?"

The pretty virologist reflected a moment and replied, "We can have a canister ready to ship by Friday."

"That's terrific, Doctor. It will keep us on schedule."

As promised, a fifty-dose vial of LOT-ONE was inside a triple-walled ceramic cylinder on the loading dock behind the mausoleum. Technicians checked for leaks, found none and gave the "high sign" to the doctor. She in turn nodded her approval to slide the canister on specially-designed rails and an automated dolly into a padded van. The colonel then instructed two armed guards to escort the world-changing payload on the overnight trip to the encapsulation facility. The guards had very clear orders: "Shoot to Kill!"

-//-

As the sun illuminated the classified medical facility built by an intelligence agency specifically for project Blue Planet, Colonel Wan could see all of the activities via a remote television hook-up with video feeds from ground systems and drones. The canister was unloaded and rolled into a containment chamber. After an integrity inspection, it was slowly rolled into the sterile high bay production room. The goal was to create the requisite capsules as soon as possible to avoid unintentional leaks. Soon employees in clean suits and oxygen helmets clustered around the equipment. A mobile robot lifted the vial out of the canister and slowly, carefully lowered it into a special receptacle at the front end of the encapsulation machine. A robot with 3-D video cameras in its eyes moved to the side of the 16-foot-long machine for the live video transmission to Beijing and Ordos. The machine operator signaled that the proper temperature had been attained in order to melt the encapsulation sheet down onto the pill mold. A flashing yellow light indicated that the process was about to begin.

A couple seconds later, the light turned red and several levers, belts and conveyors feed the material into the mold chamber and released a tray of fifty pellets on a blister sheet. The machine operator switched off the assembly line and gave the "thumbs-up" sign. To the onlookers, the process was over almost before it started! Watching the video in Ordos, Colonel Wan reminded himself that such machines routinely make hundreds of thousands of pills in a run. He called Dr. Cho, who was also watching the video feed, to confirm that the next step was to place the blister pack into a canister for transport to Shenzhen. As the video feed closed, technicians could be seen spraying the machine with a hot disinfectant.

-//-

The next morning the special van was escorted by several military vehicles as it entered the Imagineering PCB manufacturing plant in Shenzhen. The company's management decided that the automated equipment would not be delicate enough for the dangerous task. Consequently, a team of Top-Secret assemblers in protective gear was ready after practicing for almost a month with a cellphone burn plate. Each capsule was gently inked with a code number and set in place using a microscope. Each placement took about ten minutes so the entire day was devoted to this classified procedure.

Once each PCB was inspected by high power cameras and sensitive sniffers in a large circular chamber, the PCB was snapped into place on the cellphone cover. Then the battery contacts were soldiered onto the card. A robot finger powered on the device and put it though a series of final assembly operational tests. After the 50 cellphones were wrapped in cellophane for retail sale, they were transferred by the robot to a secure, locked chamber. That evening the chamber was placed in a large, ceramic-lined, leak-proof metal box for the midnight convoy to Ordos.

6

Choibalsan

While the metal box was being unloaded at the virology laboratory in Ordos, Dr. Cho personally monitored the sensor panel for any leaks. Satisfied the cargo was intact, she went to her office and made two telephone calls. On a secure line, she contacted two entities in the small northern city of Choibalsan. This central Mongolian city is one of the most remote on Earth. Located almost 600 miles north of Ordos, the city's name is very revealing: "Bad Water and Desert." No crops can grow there, and the 2,500 residents endure frequent sandstorms.

One of her calls was to a small medical clinic being refurbished to serve the town.

"Hello, Dr. Sun, this is Dr. Cho in Ordos. Are you ready to conduct the tests we talked about last month?"

"Yes, doctor, we are ready, and the supplies you requested are here in my office."

"Very well, sir, we will arrive late tomorrow. Please reserve six rooms in the military barracks for me and my team."

"Will do. And please be assured that nobody, I mean NOBODY, knows of your visit and mission."

"As usual, Thank You, sir! You are a real CCP comrade!"

The second call she made was to the local prison in Choibalsan, a stark cinder block facility housing three-dozen political prisoners. The doctor had a vision of a Gulag in Siberia as she waited for the warden to come to the phone.

"Dr. Cho," said Warden Fun-so, "glad to hear your voice. We are ready and assigned twenty-four inmates to your important task."

"Thank you, sir, you are most professional! We will arrive late tomorrow with our team and supplies for the three days of tests."

"Doctor, we're ready to serve your mission. If I remember correctly, you called it "Blue Planet.""

"You're right, sir. I look forward to finally meeting you and very successful tests. Goodbye."

-//-

In Ordos, Colonel Wan supervised the loading of the canister into an airtight rail car with two armed guards. The overnight train was the only one to serve the city of Choibalsan. Early the next morning, Dr. Cho, Colonel Wan and two technicians and two safety officers started the 14-hour flight to Choibalsan with a layover in Altay, Mongolia. A military convoy picked up the team for the 60-mile trip east to the "End of the Earth."

-//-

AT 7:30 the next morning, the team was welcomed at the clinic and escorted to a small conference room. Dr. Cho briefed several medical personnel: "We have a 3 eight-person work groups assigned to the tests. One test will be performed each day to check the results and assure our safety. "Is the necessary monitoring equipment set up and functioning properly?"

"Yes, doctor, they are just as you ordered."

She then turned to Colonel Wan, "Colonel, are all of your people briefed and ready?"

"Yes, doctor, they are, and we will be supplemented by prison guards and ambulance personnel."

"Excellent, Colonel. Your preparations are critical to this endeavor and truly appreciated," replied the slight, but dominating, virologist.

The group then synchronized their watches as the doctor said, "It's a go!"

An hour later, eight prisoners were led into the clinic, handed paint brushes and given assignments to white wash the walls of the infirmary. In the background, the conference room was readied per the Doctor's instructions.

Exactly at noon, the work party was ordered to take a break in the conference room to receive a telephone call from the President congratulating them on their "freedom from their daily worries!"

As each prisoner was led into the room, he was handed a cellphone to take the congratulatory call. When they were all seated at the table and drinking hot tea, Dr. Cho left the room to "coordinate the President's call." As she closed the airtight door, she instructed the group to each press the power button on the cellphone and put it up to their ears for the important call. Only 2-seconds later, a recording of the President's voice said: "Your sentence is hereby commuted and good luck in your new world. Good-bye."

Within seconds, and almost simultaneously, the eight men slumped over the table as several cellphones fell to the floor. Dr. Cho and her team pulled back a curtain over a window on the side of the room. No words were spoken. No one in the room was alive. The virologist took a deep breath and gave the sign for the special ventilation equipment to be turned on to evacuate any residual vapors in the room. The twenty-minute process ended with an "all clear' signal via lights and buzzers. Two ambulances were backed up to the front door of the clinic. The technicians from Ordos in their safety suits, looking almost like astronauts, entered the conference room and checked the pulse of each person. The "high sign" was given, and they began to collect the cellphones and carry the bodies to the ambulance. Fifteen minutes later, the vehicles were on their way to an abandoned coal mine shaft.

Over the next two hours, all of the data capture devices were checked and their contents saved on remote devices. The conference room was sealed and filled with neutralization sanitation gas to remain overnight to completely ensure its effectiveness. At 4:00 pm, the colonel saluted the doctor as they got into vehicles for the ride back to the military compound. Nobody could see the grin of satisfaction coming over Dr. Cho's face as she starred at the dusty plains.

-//-

The entire test regime was repeated on each of the following two days. A total of 24 prisoners were congratulated. All of the phones were collected and placed in a sealed steel box at the national strategic metals dump twenty-four miles east of the city. The prevailing wind always blows toward the coastal city of Vladivostok in Russia.

The Ordos team completed the sanitation of the conference room. The warden confirmed the disappearance of the bodies. And the colonel reminded his men of the Top-Secret nature of the mission as the trucks rolled south to Ordos.

There was no time for celebration. Dr. Cho was driven to Almay to catch a plane to Ordos. During the flight, she outlined her report to Beijing using a codeword dictionary she had memorized. A couple times during the flight, she broke into a cold sweat worried about an accidental release of the virus which was more lethal than any other on Earth. It replicated at record speed, and there were no antibodies. She thought to herself: "I bet this is how the Swede Nobel felt when he realized the impact of dynamite on civilization."

7

Beijing II

Two weeks later, the Ordos team was in the lobby of the Government Employee Hotel in the Middle Sea section of the Forbidden City. Dr. Cho reviewed her notes out loud and confirmed that each person knew exactly what their assignment was in the coming meeting. Promptly at 8:30AM a van arrived to take them to the nearby Shanghai Peoples Government Office Building where they could brief the President in a secure lower basement vault where cellphones were not allowed.

About twenty people crowded in the vault and were instructed on the protocol when the President arrived. Colonel Wan gave Dr. Cho the "high sign" for confidence. The participants were from Admirals to Tower construction company executives and many skills in between. The president of the capsule company smiled at the doctor and gave her a "thumbs-up" sign.

A few minutes later, everyone rose to their feet as President Ling entered the room. He looked around the room, smiled and gestured for everyone to take their seat. After a sip of tea, the Chief of Staff went around the room and introduced everyone, all hand-picked by him. His bottom line was: A Go-No Go decision about the final stage of Operation Blue Planet. Everyone in the vault knew the importance of the decision for the Chinese, indeed, mankind on Earth.

Dr. Cho gave the first briefing about the development of the toxic virus. She highlighted the proof of its lethality with videos from Choibalsan. Many questions were asked about the safe-handling of the containers. Colonel Wan assured the group that the military had proven procedures and trained soldiers to handle them regardless of the mode of transportation.

The next briefing was by the President of Shimbao. Several slides showed the encapsulation process and requisite safety actions. He thanked the President for his foresight to build the new, classified facility.

Then the General Manager from Imagineering gave a short overview of the PCB manufacturing process showing the extreme care used to place the viral capsule near the microphone mouthpiece of the cellphone. He ended his remarks by assuring the audience that his company could produce all of the special cellphones the nation needed.

A short bio-break then preceded the joint briefing by the Economics Minister and the Debt Trap Program Manager. The major infrastructure projects in foreign countries financed by China trapped the host nations with high debt which they hoped would be forgiven. It was often forgiven in exchange for the Chinese sole ownership of the national communications system. The audience was impressed how quickly major projects were planned and executed at strategic locations around the globe. Only 3 of the 22 were not completed, and they were not critical to the completion of the Blue Planet project. Some of the key projects included:

- Military base and port in Ethiopia (to guard the Suez Canal)
- Military base in Venezuela (to guard the Panama Canal)
- Port and Base in Morocco (to guard the Straits of Gibraltar)
- Ports and Bases on artificial islands surrounding China's mainland (and control Taiwan as necessary)
- Complete the Artic Waterway in northern Russia (sea route between Atlantic and Pacific Oceans)
- Military outpost on the Moon
- Ring of communications and geolocation satellites around the equator and in Polar orbit
- Control sea supply chains
- Telecommunications towers in Iran. Palestine and Russia for television, radio and cellular telephone

President Ling smiled when the briefer answered the last question and sat down. He then motioned for the Chief to summarize the situation for decision purposes. The Chief was quite confident when he spoke:

- We control the oceans, canals and waterborne supply chains
- We have the largest fleet of nuclear submarines
- We have the largest army ever trained
- We have the stealth hypersonic aircraft
- We have the largest arsenal of nuclear-tipped missiles in missile-proof bunkers and mountain caves
- We control space with many classified assets on orbit and on the moon
- We are owed trillions of dollars which could be paid in gold
- Our viruses have forced global shut downs resulting in destroyed economies and democratic republics forcing the establishment of Communist States
- Now we have a lethal cellphone which can control or eliminate key people around the globe

My President and Standing Committee members, I, therefore, believe that we are positioned to execute the last element of the Blue Planet project. I request your approval to proceed on behalf of our Peoples to gain global control."

The seven members of the Standing Committee seated at the table each nodded their consent. The President looked around the room and asked: "Is there any more information we need in order to make a decision? (The silence was deafening.)

President Ling then rose to his feet and in a very powerful voice said: "Hearing none, it shall be done! Proceed with the successful completion of project Blue Planet by the end of the next two moon cycles."

Everyone in the room stood up as the President turned around and left the vault. Dr. Cho and Colonel Wan's eyes met as if to say: "I was part of the biggest decision in world history."

8

Hong Kong

After a night of good French wine and sexual bliss under the covers, a Chinese-American couple enjoyed hot coffee the next morning on the balcony of their apartment at 15 Conduit Road overlooking the central business district of Hong Kong.

The foreign service couple had often been awarded for twenty years of accurate reporting about China. Mi Lan Po and her Life Partner, Andrew Ho, have a network of clandestine and loyal reporters throughout the mainland and on Taiwan. The data gets to the couple in a wide variety of classified means, many of which are unknown to even the Ambassador.

"Andrew, I'm really concerned about the Chinese takeover of the planet. As if the takeover of this city in 1999 when the British lease expired wasn't enough, they now control all countries except for a few which are not worth the effort like Australia and India. And, of course, what has become of America is the greatest national transformation in history. In a couple decades, the United States of America (USA) has become the United Socialist Republic (USR). This is the largest fall of a political entity since the Roman Empire."

"My dear, you know I share you anger," replied the 45-year-old internationally-acclaimed architect. After a sip of coffee, he started counting on his fingers:

- Largest lethal military force in history
- Total control of the oceans
- Unchallenged control of the global supply chains
- Control of the financial markets through Debt Traps (even to America), currencies and gold.
- The CCP knows and controls the whereabouts of every citizen Indeed, we need to be super cautious or the authorities will be knocking on our door!"

"Have you heard something new which has you so concerned?"

"Honey," replied Mi Lan, "a couple of trusted sources have reported events in Ordos, Mongolia and Beijing, which when taken together, are really scary!"

"What do you mean?"

"Well, they moved the military virology laboratory to Ordos. There has been a dramatic increase in activity there. Last week a convoy was seen leaving there for Outer Mongolia. Recently, the principals were seen boarding a plane for Beijing.

Something's happening, but I haven't put the pieces together yet. It may be nothing. But I dare not report it to Washington; it's too risky."

"Well, if anybody can ferret out the truth, it's you, my dear!"

"Thanks, honey. It's almost time for our appointment downtown. Have you forgotten?"

"Are you kidding? Who would ever miss the delivery of a wristwatch at a Patek Philippe boutique?"

They both smiled as they went to the door with umbrellas in hand.

9

Tehran

As the new communications tower was being completed at the Pods Telecommunication Center in the University District of Tehran, Iran, China quietly moved its forces into tactical positions. Fifty thousand Afghani "volunteers" were amassed on the Iranian border 60-miles east of the city of Mashhad where Highway 22 enters Afghanistan at "Sovietjab."

An aircraft carrier and escort vessels took their positions just off Bushehr Port on the Persian Gulf. A convoy of flatbed trucks carrying tanks moved through Turkmenistan toward the northeast border of the country.

In the northernmost section of the country, once the famous Persian empire, a second tower was recently completed in the city of Rasht. The Chinese construction crew was given bonuses for their project. The transmitters are two hundred feet above the city are so powerful the signal can be heard from Rome to Mumbai. Unknown to the Iranians, most of the broadcast channels were reserved for the Chinese military.

As the Tehran Tower was undergoing its final testing, and the paperwork being submitted to the Iranian authorities, the station management was in contact with Beijing to coordinate an upcoming event. The management was also in daily contact with a small group of Chinese at the university. Led by a history professor, this group of six men was hand-picked by Beijing to serve as a shadow government for the country of Iran.

Early on a Sunday morning, a military cargo plane landed at the Tehran International Airport and taxied to the national guard side of the field. A convoy of five trucks met the plane. Within twenty minutes, a large crate marked "Medical Supplies" was forklifted onto one of the trucks. It was no accident that all of the men in the convoy were Chinese. On deserted streets the convoy rolled up to the loading dock of the Tower's new office building.

"Is everything in order?" asked the Stationmaster.

"Yes, sir, it is. Your package is safe and ready for use," replied the convoy commander.

Early Monday morning, the Chinese Embassy informed the Iranian Department of State that President Ling would like to personally christen the new Tehran Tower using new cellphones with the Ayatollah and his close staff of seven mullahs in a conference room at the Grand Mosque across the boulevard from university park. As an inducement to participate in the call, the Chinese leaked the idea that the President was going to forgive billions of dollars in Debt Trap financing. "A new Era of Harmony" was about to begin in Iran."

-//-

A light snow was falling as the clergy were finishing their Saturday services throughout the capital city. The candles still burned in the Grand Mosque as the Ayatollah Ali Khamenei signaled to his top advisors to join him in the basement conference room to take the call from President Ling. The public never saw this room with its antique silk Persian carpets and fixtures of pure gold.

Staff members bowed obediently as the group entered the room. The Ayatollah took his seat at the end of the long conference table flanked by three men on each side. At the other end of the table was a video screen showing a live view of Beijing's Forbidden City. A countdown clock in the upper right corner was counting down from five minutes.

Outside the mosque, a military convoy of four trucks and two black SUVs pulled up to the underground loading dock. Plain clothes guards accompanied a large metal case as it rolled past security once the passes of the Tower staff were validated. The leader of the group used a key to unlock the case positioned just outside the conference room.

Given the nod of approval, he took a tray of cellphones out of the case and placed the individual phones on a gold platter. With one-minute left on the countdown clock, two men placed the platter on the table in front of the Ayatollah who nodded permission for the distribution of the phones around the table. Only seconds later President Ling appeared on the video screen. The recording started with a greeting in Farci and congratulations for the new telecommunications infrastructure. "I wish to convey an important message," started the President. "To prove the effectiveness and capabilities of the new system, even in a basement, please press the red power button and lift the phone to your ear."

The congratulatory atmosphere quickly turned into a horror scene as one-by-one the men slumped down on the table and dropped their cellphones on the floor. The guards were immediately subdued and the room sealed off. The team leader then called the convoy.

A couple minutes later, special filter fans were rolled up to the door to evacuate the poison vapor from the room. After 10 minutes, the green light on the appliance flashed indicating that it was clear to enter the room. The cellphones were carefully placed in a sealed metal box and carried out to the trucks. This was the signal for the Shadow Government men to leave the SUVs to enter an adjoining room where a cable led from a video camera out to an antenna on one of the vehicles parked outside the building. The antenna link to the new Tower was confirmed, and the "GO" signal was relayed to the conference room.

With the "all clear" signal, the dead men were taken to the SUVs while the Chinese professor stepped to the microphone to calmly announce that a new government had been formed "to bring harmony and prosperity to the Proud Persian People." Only the Intelligencia with access to foreign news outlets knew the true meaning of the announcement: Complete Control by the Communists in Beijing.

The sailors in formation on the deck of the aircraft carrier cheered loudly. Indeed, they could almost hear the soldiers at the Afghan border, almost 800-miles away, cheer as well. In Beijing, the Chief informed the President of the success of the operation. The president put his cup of tea down, smiled and quietly said: "One more to go."

10

Hong Kong II

"**A**ndrew, what does that new watch of yours tell us what time it is?"

"6:00 PM on the dot," replied the famous architect.

"Good, let's watch the Evening News," replied the super spook.

The couple than toasted with their wine glasses and walked into the living room to click on the television.

They were just in time to hear the lead story about the change of government in Iran. "Details are sketchy, but the Ayatollah and his key advisors have not been seen in the last few days. And a Chinese national, Xi-Xi Ping, made a short, televised announcement asking for calm and the support of the new government. And the elections scheduled for next month will be postponed."

Mi Lan reacted violently, "Postponed, HELL, cancelled forever!"

Andrew looked at this partner and nodded his agreement.

"How did they pull off a bloodless coup in such a saber-rattling country?" asked Mi Lin rhetorically.

It only took a minute for the couple to reflect upon the strategic importance of the takeover for China. Looking at a Google Map on a tablet, it was clear to them that China had gained:

- Access to the Caspian Sea
- Ports on the Persian Gulf
- Tactical proximity to the Suez Canal
- Advanced missile systems to threaten Israel and Saudi Arabia
- A strong, math-oriented technology culture
- A long border with Afghanistan and tactical border with Turkey
- Oil and Gas reserves

The pretty woman stood up, walked over to the sliding glass door to the balcony, looked out at her beloved city, paused a moment and said, "Andrew, I bet a Debt Trap had something to do with this."

"I bet you're right, my dear. The CCP invested billions in their infrastructure and wanted payment for their notes just like they've done in Africa and the Americas."

"Andrew, I'm going to look into this, I feel that somehow advanced tactical communications systems are involved.

And, my guess, and it's only a guess, is that the Iranians are dead. The Chinese would never allow a state funeral where the sympathetic, religious zealots would march and riot. And you've got to believe they've got military assets surrounding the country to squash any rebellion if necessary."

"Right again, my dear. This all happened over a weekend. How could they have pulled it off without a lot of prior planning?"

-//-

The couple was too agitated to cook dinner so Andrew ordered take out and poured more wine. Mi Lan studied a world map on her tablet and asked, "What does this mean for global geopolitics?" She counted on her fingers:

- With America now a Socialist Republic (aka Communist Country) and its treasury drained by the welfare programs, the country can no longer be the World's Policeman. Therefore, countries like Canada, Mexico, Japan, South Korea, Saudi Arabia and all of central Europe can no longer count on Uncle Sam for protection from China or Russia.
- The countries of Africa and South America were already trapped by debt to the Chinese
- Australia's too isolated to impact global affairs
- India is only a huge liability which nobody wants

So, when you look at the map, there's only one more target for China to control the world: Russia. And, Andrew, as you know, the Chinese are already heavily invested in there Artic Waterway and advance telecommunications systems."

Andrew took a sip of wine and added: "Honey, you're right. The Chinese don't need their vodka but would want to control their nuclear arsenal, access to the Baltic Sea and the wheat fields of the Steppe. It would be a logical next target."

"I think we need to do some digging and quickly pulse our friends about out preliminary conclusion," said Mi Lan.

"And there's the big question: "How long will it be before Democracies can again flourish on Earth, if ever?" asked Andrew. "What event(s) will force global Communism to implode as it always has in history? Where will the spark originate?"

"Well, my love, even if you had the answers, who would you call? Beijing's in charge here and would listen to the call and soon knock on our door!"

11

Moscow

"Welcome, Sir, we've been expecting you," said the security guard as the Chief put his valise on the conveyor belt.

"Thank you, sir. Please escort me to the conference room. I'm chilled to the bone and need some tea…something stronger if you have it!"

"Yes, Sir, please follow me." After an elevator ride down to a subbasement and a short walk down a dingy hall with murals of Ukrainian peasants on both walls, the Chief entered the secure room. He was immediately greeted by the Ambassador and Station Chief and their staffs. The Ambassador then introduced a three-person telecommunications team which recently completed a state-of-the-art tower complex only one mile from the Kremlin and a gift from the People of China. The last person to be introduced was a virologist handpicked by Dr. Cho for this important mission.

The Station Chief served as the Project Leader and developed the briefing for the Chief. Nobody bull-shits the Chief! If they do, they disappear. First to brief was the Tower Project Manager who summarized the new communications technology stolen from the USR to be used commercially and for military purposes. The Chief asked a lot of questions, all of which were answered quickly and with precision.

Then an Intelligence Officer briefed about the military deployments in preparation for the cellphone demonstration. These preparations included:

- Military convoy on the Silk Road, ready to take up a position only 300-miles east of Moscow
- Aircraft carrier flotilla in the Baltic Sea
- Stealth aircraft in Iran
- Spies in the Kremlin's spy Agency (KGB) ready to assume control

"So, Chief, we have over 100,000 men and their equipment ready for any emergency," said the Station Chief with real pride in his voice."

The last to speak was the virologist who confirmed:

- Readiness status of the cellphones
- Safety and security measures in place

- Completion of two rehearsals as shown on a video
- Post event sensing procedures and sanitation measures

The Chief than asked for a copy of the President's address to be broadcast. He read it and nodded his approval.

"Sir, that completes our briefing; we await your authorization to proceed."

The Chief looked around the room, clapped his hands in appreciation of the briefings and said: "I will be in touch by 5:00PM on Thursday.

-//-

Promptly at 1:00PM, the Chief and his principal, trusted interpreter were ushered into the Russian President's outer office. They were there only a couple minutes before the President entered the room and warmly welcomed his guests. At a round table in front of the President's ornately carved desk, the Chief summarized his visit:

- Commission of the Tower Complex
- Review of the troops at the Moscow Barracks
- The delivery of the Note to the National Bank forgiving the debt for the new complex"

President Kolzou had a huge grin on his face as he reached across the table to shake the Chief's hand.

The Chief then said: "Sir, I have one small request."

"Oh, what's that, Sir?"

"I request that you and your top advisors honor my country by personally receiving a message from President Ling on your new, very advanced, cellphones."

"Of course," replied the President, who then said: "Oh, now I see that my calendar shows the telecon early Friday morning."

The Chief nodded and ended his short visit by politely refusing a vodka toast and wishing Moscow success in the new Era of Harmony.

In the bitter cold, the Chief's car drove across Red Square to the famous Breguet Boutique to shop for a new wristwatch and an anniversary necklace to celebrate a half-century of marital bliss.

On Thursday evening, the Chief sipped a Manhattan cocktail in front of the fireplace in his suite as he phoned his secretary to say: "Operation Blue Planet is a GO."

-//-

At 7:00AM on Friday, the Project Manager confirmed the readiness of the military assets as two technicians and safety officer loaded the ceramic-lined metal case into a black van.

He then called the Security Office at the Kremlin to confirm his arrival for the 8:00 AM meeting with the President and his advisors in the basement conference room. The request was approved.

The President was all smiles as announced to his staff the forgiveness of the debt for the new telecommunications station. All of his eight cabinet members were delighted, and their staffs were told to return in an hour.

Just before the meeting, the case was rolled to the conference room and the Leader confirmed the readiness of the assets waiting in the garage. The Chief's Secretary asked for the case to be opened to check the contents who then nodded his approval to the Chief. The Chief was then announced and entered the room with a cordial welcome from President Kolzou and his ministers. As he carefully handed each person a cellphone, he warned not to power it on until President Ling appears on the video screen at the end of the table. He then smiled, bowed as a courtesy gesture and left the room. Only seconds later, through a remote speaker in the antechamber, he could hear the introduction of President Ling. At that moment, the two Chinese technicians chloroformed the two guards by thrusting soaked washcloths over their faces. They fell to the floor and were dragged to the awaiting convoy.

In the meantime, President Ling's message continued: "My esteemed Comrades, it is an honor to present Russia with this new technology. It is offered as a token of Friendship and

Harmony between our two nations. Please press the RED button and put the phone up to your ear to hear the rest of my important message for the Russian People."

All nine men followed the direction, and within seconds, one-by-one, to the horror of the others, they slumped over the table. The Chief was quickly escorted out to the Convoy to confirm the event and que up a recording to be broadcast to the nation via the new Tower. Five minutes passed before one of the technicians was allowed to enter the room in an astronaut-like safety suit. He confirmed the death of everyone as he picked up the cellphones for confinement in a special case. On his que, the Chief pressed the button on the recorder:

"Comrades, I am pleased to announce that we have a change in our government. Our new leaders will be address you on Monday. To honor the Russian People and this important event, this weekend is declared a National Holiday to celebrate the New Era of friendship and prosperity."

As the van pulled out of the garage, two military ambulances entered to retrieve the corpses and sanitize the room. Once the area was declared vapor-free, the vehicles sped away to dispose of their cargoes through a hole in the ice on the Volga River. The decomposed bodies might be found many months later with the spring thaw.

In the meantime, the Chief warmed himself in the new Tower Control Center breakroom with a cup of hot coffee. It was only 15-minutes later when he was handed a cellphone.

"Are you sure this phone is OK to use? (Ha-Ha)

The Project Manager called from the side of the river to inform his boss that "Operation Blue Planet "(Lan SeXingqiu) was completed.

On a very secure line, the Chief called his boss to report the good news.

12

New York City

All of New York's newspapers and evening news reports were about the new Chinese leadership in Moscow. It was still a mystery of the whereabouts of the President and his cabinet. Pictures in the papers showed troops marching across Red Square for a review by Chinese leadership. Soon, too many questions needed answers. The Secretary General of the United Nations was forced to call a Special Session of the Security Council. Because China was busy assuming complete control of Russia, the ambassador asked for a two-week delay which was granted.

On a cold February day with sleet pelting the UN Headquarters building, delegations began to arrive for a noon meeting of the Security Council. The USR Ambassador was a Chinese National. At 11:00 AM, the Ghanian Secretary General was told of the Chinese delegation arrival on a Hypersonica commercial jet from Beijing. The mood of the diplomatic corps could only be described as "Abject Fear!"

The council members, representing 16 nations, all of whom were deeply in debt to or controlled by China, awaited the Beijing delegation under Foreign Minister Sow Gun Man. No one at the United Nations could imagine what was to happen next. After the roll call, the German Ambassador requested an explanation from the Chinese about the recent coup in Russia.

"We demand, Sir, an explanation as this act appears to be counter to the charter of this body and may require sanctions."

All eyes were on the elder Chinese stateman who rose to his feet and in fluent English announced:

"Since the majority of the membership of this body owe their existence to my nation, I bring to you a proclamation from President Ling. It reads as follows:

"Henceforth and forever more, the United Nations shall cease to exist. It serves no useful purpose in the People's World. Therefore, this building, and any other structures and organizations of any type used to conduct the business of the United Nations are hereby closed."

Everyone in attendance gasped!

The diplomat continued:

"I inform you that all current funds of any kind in or for this organization are now the property of the National Bank of China."

The gasps grew louder!

"Gentlemen, be it further understood that all committees, panels, councils, working groups anywhere on Earth are hereby eliminated. This includes all commissions, including but not limited to:

- Disarmament
- Human Rights
- International Trade and Export Regulations
- Peace Building (Forces Disbanded and equipment transferred to the People's Army)
- Relief Services
- Law and Ethics
- Global Warming

Therefore, since the organization no longer exists, and you and your staffs have no business here, the People's Republic has arranged immediate transportation back to your home country. All files and documents of any kind in any media are now the property of my country and must remain in place here and everywhere on Earth.

As you exit this room, you will be given the appropriate travel voucher for ground and air transportation. Each of you has three (3) hours to board your flight. The security forces in this city belong to us and will assist with your departure. In your country, as I speak, the United Nations offices are being closed and all materials confiscated.

No remuneration of any kind will be forthcoming during this evacuation. After today, United Nations' passports are no longer valid."

Grasps, groans and outright sobbing filled the chamber.

"So, my new Comrades, soldiers in the People's Army, you are ordered to leave this room peaceably. Resistance is futile. Any such actions will result in the incarceration of your family members. Indeed, stragglers will be incarcerated without due process of law. United Nations privileges no longer apply."

-//-

Everyone who had a cellphone was either making a call or receiving one. "Are you serious? How could this be happening?" In the background, the Chinese delegation was surrounded by Mongolian storm tropers and escorted to the exit.

-//-

This action was the second to last in the checklist for the completion of the Blue Planet project. On the hypersonica flight back to Beijing, the Ambassador enjoyed an adult beverage and was heard to say: "I hope they like the Chinese language."

13

Beijing III

During the first week of March, President Ling assembled his staff to discuss Lessons Learned from Operation Blue Planet and near-term actions. The Chief had already asked for ideas from the key staff members. Many of the ideas were listed on the tablet in front of each minister. Key lessons learned included:

- Global Socialism (Communism when militant actions are taken against the citizens) is the norm because people want to be led by a central force
- Large militaries are required to control the masses and provide disguised unemployment
- Modern technologies are effective tools to spy on the people
- Nations have no way out of Debt Traps

- The planet is three-quarters water; therefore, control of the oceans for commerce and military actions is essential
- Cybersecurity is critical in a world funded by cryptocurrency
- The next wars will be in space; plan for it
- Virology is a two-headed monster which can help or hurt mankind

As the last one came up on the screen, the President smiled and said: "Comrades Operation Blue Planet used a virus effectively, but now we've created a monster which we must slay."

The ministers looked at each other with blank expressions on their faces. "What does he mean?"

The Chief was quick to answer the question: "We no longer need the Cellphonica to control the world. It's simply too risky to continue these Gain-of-Function programs. Our leader directs us to close our 4 virology laboratories. Remember the accident in Wuhan. It killed over 6 million people by infecting only one person who got on an airplane. We will keep only one civilian laboratory open to control diseases here or elsewhere around the world we now control.

-//-

One week later, Dr. Cho and Colonel Wan entered the Great Hall in Forbidden City. They walked down the red carpet with the Chief. They stopped just in front of the President. Staff members and court reporters entered the hall. In a loud, bellowing voice, President Ling asked Dr. Cho to come forward. She took a position on the red line as directed.

"Dr. Cho, your efforts on behalf of our Peoples have been extraordinary. You are to be congratulated by relinquishing your leadership of the laboratory in Ordos. This facility will be permanently closed as well as the other three laboratories controlled by the military. As of this moment, you are now the Director of a new facility in the Shenzhen Medical Research Park. Your staff will research only medicinal uses of spike protein molecules. China thanks you. Go forward, and may you flourish on behalf of our People."

The woman bowed in gratitude and walked back to her spot next to the colonel.

"Colonel Wan, please step forward."

With a respectful military gait, the man came forward to hear his fate. The President got a small box from a staff member.

"Colonel, your leadership was instrumental in the success of the Blue Planet mission. Here is your star that you shall proudly wear as a general officer in the People's Army. Your first task, which I believe you'll accept, is to close our military virology laboratories. You must do so with absolute safety that no pathogens whatsoever are released in any form. Do you understand, Sir?"

"I understand and will comply, SIR!"

The President continued: "My staff has researched and selected the Tamir Gol mine in central Mongolia for the repository of all of the equipment, samples and related supplies. This abandoned iron mine, which has a thousand-foot shaft in the middle of the sparest region on Earth, appears ideal for the disposal. Sir, you have 6-months to complete the task and report such to me. Congratulations from your Countrymen and women!"

The new general officer turned around, smiled at Dr. Cho and returned to his original position.

"Chief, please periodically report the progress of both of their tasks to me. I consider them one of my highest priorities which must be successfully completed on schedule. Do I make myself clear?'

"Yes, Sir!"

14

Tamir Gol

The new general quickly went into action. He assigned a Task Leader and a company-level team at each of the 4 locations. From his office in Ordos, he transmitted procedures, instructions, and safety regulations for handling the infectious materials. He commissioned special trucks to be outfitted with shock absorbing containment vessels suitable for the long journey north to central Mongolia. His focus was on the preparations and processes at Ordos to serve as a model to be repeated at the other sites. He leaned heavily on his mentor and friend, Dr. Cho, who, herself, had a very busy agenda and frequent trips to Shenzhen to complete her new assignment.

One morning at the daily briefing, a serviceman asked a question: "Sir, where do you want the high-pressure hoses set up?"

General Wan was quick to answer, "Soldier, wherever there are pieces of equipment we can't autoclave. We will decontaminate with a heated hydrogen peroxide solution and dry with large fans. Portable aerosol sensors will be used to ensure the cleanliness. That is a good question which raises the steps considered critical. Here's a short list:

- Refrigerators and freezers must be tapped shut. They will be OK for the 10-hour journey.
- Gas cylinders and cryogenic liquid dewars must be moved via dolly to the trucks. No rolling of tanks will be permitted.
- All body parts must be covered at all times.
- Two-person teams rehearse every move. There will be no "Macho Men" on my watch
- All cleaned biological equipment must carry a Hazard Tag
- Containers with animal carcasses must be vacuum-sealed and labeled
- No waste is left behind. Everything; I mean Everything, will be taken
- The entire laboratory will be sanitized and sealed with no entry points. Vapor sensors will be automatically interrogated hourly to ensure no hazardous materials, however, small, will escape

Once the safety team certifies the aerosol particle count, the facility will be sealed and never available for another use."

One month to the day, the convoy of 30-trucks, with one carrying the unused cellphones, was ready to depart. On a clear Sunday morning, the convoy started north. Several miles later, the general received a message that the building was permanently sealed with all sensors operational. He then radioed the lead vehicle, "Sargent, when we get to the Mongolian border, do not stop. We just got the clearance from Beijing."

-//-

Ten hours and twenty-six minutes later, the convoy entered the mine's property and followed a dusty road six miles to the closed mine. When the general arrived, he did three things:

- Deployed a Military Police unit around the site to refuse entry
- Set up a laser to confirm the depth of the mine shaft
- Confirmed the readiness of the sealing equipment

He called his superior officer, a four-star general in Beijing, to report the status and receive the order to proceed. A two-word coded message arrived: "Deployment Approved."

The unloading and dumping the entire laboratory contents went smoothly without incident. Just before sunset, the sealant vehicle rolled up to the mine. Soon hot ceramic slurry was pumped down the shaft. Temperature sensors confirmed the hardening of the stone mixture. By 9:00 PM, the mine officials certified that the mine was sealed, leakproof and could never be re-opened. At 10:00 the convoy circled its trucks out on the steppe plain just below the mine. The circle provided limited shelter from the blowing sand for some of the vehicles, including the general's communications trailer.

The general sent a message: "Unit One secure; everyone safe." The reply was short: "Good Job. Apply same procedures to the other sites and report to me."

Four months later, the general completed the closures and got his new orders in person in Beijing: "You will join a team decommissioning nuclear sites in captive countries in our empire. Your first duty assignment will be in North Dakota in the USR. Good Luck."

15

Geneva

"Ms. Shiller, Ambassador Sow Gun Man is here to see you," said the secretary to the Director General of the United Nations Office in Geneva (UNOG) in Switzerland.

"Thank you, Monika, please show him in," replied the seasoned diplomat from Germany.

They greeted each other in English and were served a cup of coffee.

"I guess you know why I'm here, Madam Secretary General," said the Chinese elder.

"Sir, I knew it was just a matter of time after what happened in New York. And I guess you're going to tell me that you have armed troops and aircraft carriers off shore to ensure everything goes smoothly."

"Yes, you are correct. The Swiss guards would be no match for my forces just across the border in Italy and France."

"Sir, not much surprises me these days!"

The ambassador began his prepared remarks: "As you may know, the Chinese People have determined that this organization is no longer of value to the world since my wonderful country controls all others except India, South Africa and Australia which are only a liability to a host country."

"I understand. What are your conditions?"

"Your organization is closed as I say these words. You and everyone else are to leave the building immediately taking only your purse or valise. Everything else must remain in place as People's property."

"Wait a minute, Ambassador Man, there is no respect or dignity in what you order!"

"There is no need for courtesies. This organization has milked its sponsors for trillions of dollars over decades with almost nothing to show for it!"

"But…"

"There's no BUT, Director General. Your commissions, conferences, councils, Institutes, and programs around the would are hereby closed. They provide no value to the billions of peasants."

"But, Sir…."

"There is no need for dialog. You are to leave the building now. We have a car downstairs to take you to your mansion. Right now, my guards are going from office to office below to escort everyone to the exits. All documents, computers and digital media must remain behind. It is now the People's Property."

As the Director General was collecting her coat and purse, the ambassador continued:

"As a show of respect to the host nation, we will pay for five (5) years lease of this campus in advance. These buildings will be hostels for refugees as well as all the buildings in your worthless empire. We will teach the refugees the joys of Communism."

As the woman was walking out of her office, she sarcastically remarked, "Oh, your president is so compassionate!"

The Chinese bureaucrat simply smiled.

Then when she was in the antechamber to her office, she saw her secretary's desk abandoned and quipped," And let me guess; NATO is next."

"You are correct. My counterpart is already there. Goodbye."

16

Hong Kong III

"Andrew, what are we going to do? Last night the phone of one of our most trusted informants in Beijing went dead. She was so close to solving how the Mullahs and Russians were killed. Now, she's probably already in transit to Mongolia, if still alive!"

"Well, my dear, that's symptomatic of the times. Let's review the situation:

- All of the important nations have been conquered by Beijing without firing a shot! Democracies are gone or doomed.
- America will soon be a Third World country
- All of the West's nuclear bombs are useless
- China controls all supply lines on the planet
- Refugee Hostels are Brainwashing Depots
- Only the Chinese currency has value (Even gold must be exchanged at a drastic discount)

- Commerce has come to a halt in many nations; no need to worry about Global Warming!
- Soon mass starvation and hordes of pestilence will be the norm"

"Ugh, Andrew, that's horrible! What can we do?"

"Oh, and I forgot. You can't escape the planet because China controls Space."

Both took a long sip of Chardonnay.

"Honey, I have a plan that just might work," said the loving partner.

"I need to get an architectural commission in Australia. We would sell this condo and move to Brisbane. We could stay with my brother until we find or build our own place."

"Andrew, that's genius! And maybe we can find a doctor who can help my mother. The procedure just might justify travel there. In a way, I'm glad my father is dead so he doesn't live this horror. It would drive him to drinking!"

"How true. Speaking of that, let's have some more wine. We can save the Dom Perignon for when I get the commission letter. Now, what's the best way to contact my brother?"

"Honey, use our special cellphone codes. The odds are calls to Australia are not being monitored."

"Yes, it's worth the risk because it's clear we can't stay here in our beloved Hong Kong."

They clinked glasses as Andrew looked Mi Lan in the eyes and said, "At least we have a glimmer of hope for the prospect of escaping, something billions of people can't dream of, much less accomplish. Life will a daily struggle to survive. And then they die. Death will be the only gift they get. Look, the rain on the window pane looks like tears to me!"

17

Bermuda

A decade before the total Communist World, American entrepreneurs established four "Micronation" island republics to preserve Democracy around the world. It was an effort to combat, or at least slow, the advance of Communism. These Micronations serve as an enclave for up to 50,000 freedom-loving and financially well-off, citizens. They were established in four regions around the world: Bermuda, Mallorca, Dubai and Singapore. They posed no threat to Beijing.

On the ground floor of the 16-story hotel serving the Micronation, Americo, across the harbor from Hamilton, Bermuda is the Federal Lounge. Today, six people are meeting to discuss the new World of China. They are:

- Win Parker, Bermuda Harbormaster and a partner in the development of the Americo Micronation

- Patrick Rosenberg, a billionaire technical genius who splits his time between Tel Aviv and Americo
- Dr. Tryg Ager, a senior director at IBM and guru in Artificial Intelligence and supercomputers
- Ben Miles, Former Director of the CIA, retired to Americo
- Evan Murray, Major General, USMC, retired
- Nancy DeYoung, Former Republican American President

Ben Miles opened the discussion with a question: "How did we lose the Democracy?"

He went around the table and then summarized the causes:

- Leaders who needed to buy votes with the unfunded promises of Socialism
- The Debt Trap; with over $10 Trillion owed to China
- Defunded military, police and first responders leading to insecurity and urban anarchy; ripe for Socialist dogma
- Technology Transfer via Student and Business Spies
- Devalued currency due to Debt and Inflation
- Export of whole industries to China
- Loss of nation's energy independence
- Use of Racism as an excuse to implement welfare programs

- Use climate concerns to divert attention from unfulfilled promises
- Opened the border to gain voters via false promises

At this point, President DeYoung spoke up: "Ben, you just named 10 reasons why I lost my job!"

"Sad, but true, Nancy," replied the savvy Spook.

"What about the Deep State agencies sabotaging your administration, afraid of losing their jobs when the swamp would be drained?" asked Ben.

"Yes, Ben, you're right."

"And I'm particularly angry about disappointing our Allies and the theft of advanced technologies," said General Murray.

"Alright, alright, you guys are depressing me. Let's plan to talk about an Action Plan tomorrow when were dining on the Aquaclipper. In the meantime, please take me up on my offer of a 10-minute Turbopod ride to Hamilton for some duty-free shopping, particularly Swiss watches. And I've reserved the Governor's Table at the Rosedon Hotel for dinner. You guys deserve 5-stars."

18

Cellphonica

The next morning, Win welcomed his friends aboard a huge Aquaclipper moored at the Americo dock. He hosted a buffet breakfast for the continuation of their discussion about the fate of democracies around the world. The goal was to develop a draft Plan of Action.

The first to speak was Dr. Ager who stated that any counter movement against China would need a secret, secure communications system to rally the forces and coordinate events.

"Tryg, you're absolutely right," said Patrick. "Do you know of a technology which we can use?"

"Yes, Patrick, I do, and it involves cellphones. Indeed, we think the Chinese poisoned the Iranian and Russian leaders by emitting a lethal vapor from a cellphone!

The group perked to hear what the IBM executive had to say.

"The cellphone is an incredible tool but can also be a potent weapon." The guru removed his cellphone from its holster and showed to the group like a magician with a deck of cards. He then powered it on, and it began to chirp like a canary.

General Murray quickly said, "I recognize that; it's Morse Code!"

"Yes, sir, it is. However, what you can't see or hear is that each chirp and the silence between them is a data store."

"What do you mean?" was the question on almost everybody's mind.

"Well, it's really quite elegant in its simplicity. You see, and Ben back me up on this, the intelligence community has for decades hidden data in the silent pauses in a telephone conversation. What this means is that when you call someone, there can be a secret data transfer within the pauses in your conversation."

Ben nodded his confirmation of the process.

"Today, this is enabled by VoIP Gateways with data-driven networks to provide multiple services like the Internet and video streaming. Some carriers have evolved the technology to bypass standard networks to provide higher quality services. Are you aware that a smartphone:

- Can be a television remote
- Check battery life of remote devices

- Store maps on line
- Stop ringing by placing your palm on the screen
- Magnify the screen with 3 taps.
- Transmit a FAX
- Store megabytes of data in a picture

"So why do I mention this? Because a cellphone can also be a taser or laser capable of immobilizing or killing a person."

"OK, Tryg, but how does this help bring back a democracy?" asked President DeYoung.

"Nancy, let me answer that by stating a few facts of life:

- We no longer are allowed to own guns of any kind
- We can't build a battleship to attack the Main land
- We can't storm the Forbidden City

Right?"

"Yes, that's right, so…?"

"So, we need a new weapon and strategy to slay the Chinese Dragon. The IBM Laboratory in Israel has created a new application which turns each smartphone into a firearm with deadly laser bursts. All that is required is a larger, more capable battery which can be purchased under the guise of supporting more memory. The laser beam is focused by the camera lens. We can sell the batteries here in the Americo store.

The second part of our plan, should we approve it, is to train a shadow Chinese Government at Malayo in Singapore. It will consist of a President, Chief of Staff, and chiefs of the treasury, military, internal affairs and foreign relations.

So, here's where the plot thickens. Every year the Chinese President and his six-person Standing Committee hold a planning offsite at the Nansha Resort on the south coast of China near Qingdao. During breaks they hold press conferences and photo opportunities for tourists in the lobby or outside by the pool.

Our trained Shadow Government will be in the tourist group. On que, when television cameras are broadcasting the event, the tourists will snap their pictures, and, presto, seven men will be dead. The new Foreign Minister will orchestrate an impromptu press conference where the new president will ask for peace. Within the hour, a Turbopod will deliver the new leaders to the President's office in Beijing.

What do you think!"

General Murray answered: "It sounds crazy, but we have NO military solution to the problem."

"How do you know the leaders will be at the resort and available?" asked Ben.

"Ben, as you know, our informers have moved from Hong Kong to Brisbane. But they have proven ways to probe their sources in China. All communications will be by background code in the silent pauses of harmless cellphone conversations. Almost daily, they contact friends in Malayo."

More questions were adroitly answered by the good Doctor before a server brought in a tray of Bald Eagle or "Baldie" cocktails. This beverage consists of 1 part Bacardi Gold rum and 2 parts Orangina with a lime wedge and spritz of whipped cream. Much like Irish Coffee, it's appropriate for the morning meeting.

President DeYoung offered a toast: "Here's to the Bald Eagle. May it once again soar over a proud Democracy in America!"